I0752997

The Magical Journey

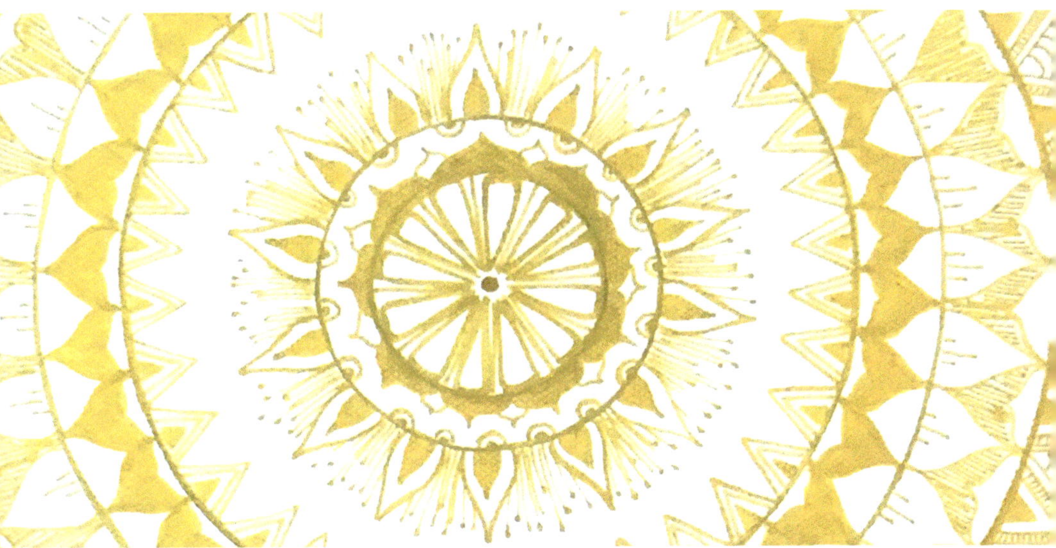

A Tale of Beauty Lost and Found

Written and Illustrated by
Dana Wheeles

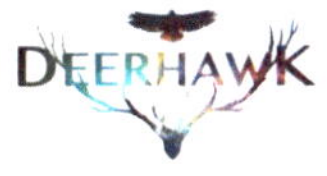

See Also:

A Gallery of Delightfully Doofy Birds, 2020

www.danawheeles.com
www.deerhawkhealing.com

Copyright Year: 2020
First Edition

ISBN: 978-1-7366015-0-1

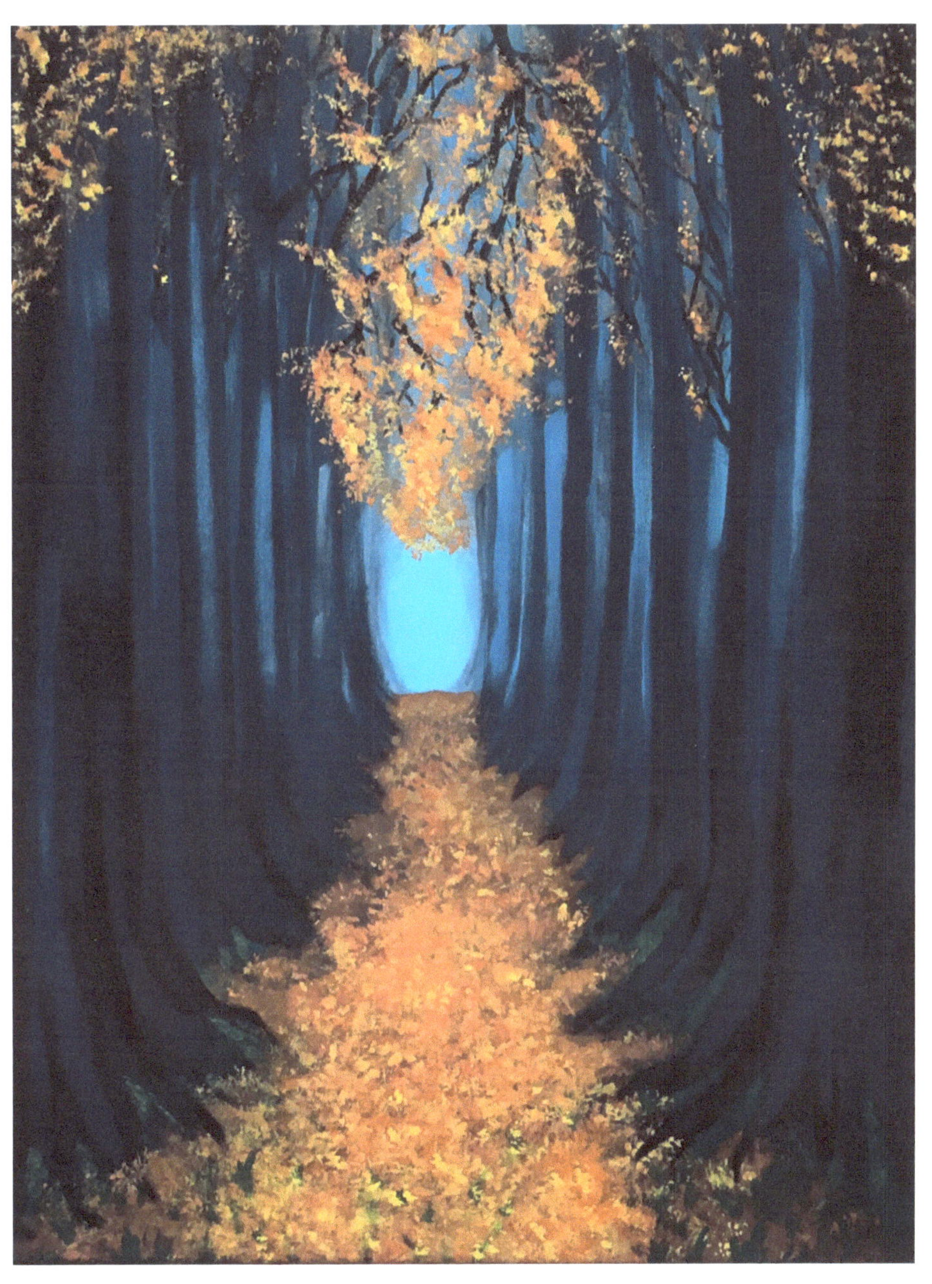

Let the journey begin. . .

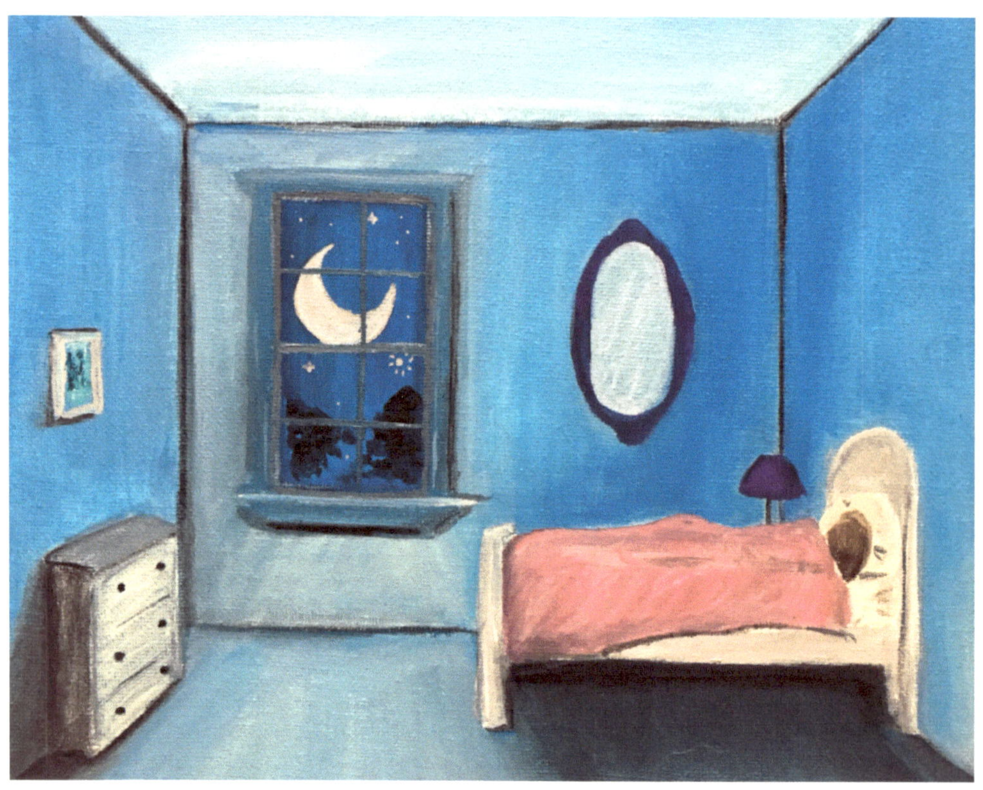

Keira was having another bad night. She tossed and turned in her bed, unable to quiet her thoughts. Life seemed so dreary lately, like an endless series of mornings and bedtimes with drudgery in between. Where had the magic of the world gone? Where was her sense of possibility?

The moon hung low in the sky and soon another day would dawn. She sighed, as tears welled in her eyes.

"I wish I could see beauty in the world again." She immediately felt sheepish as her words echoed off of the walls of her room. She was too old for things like beauty and magic. She closed her eyes and cried, feeling lost and alone.

When she re-opened her eyes, the room seemed brighter. She sat up, thinking the sun was rising. The light, however, did not come from her window.

Rather, it came from below it, in the shape of a shimmering golden ball. She rubbed her eyes, wiping them dry of tears. Indeed, there was something glowing at the foot of her bed!

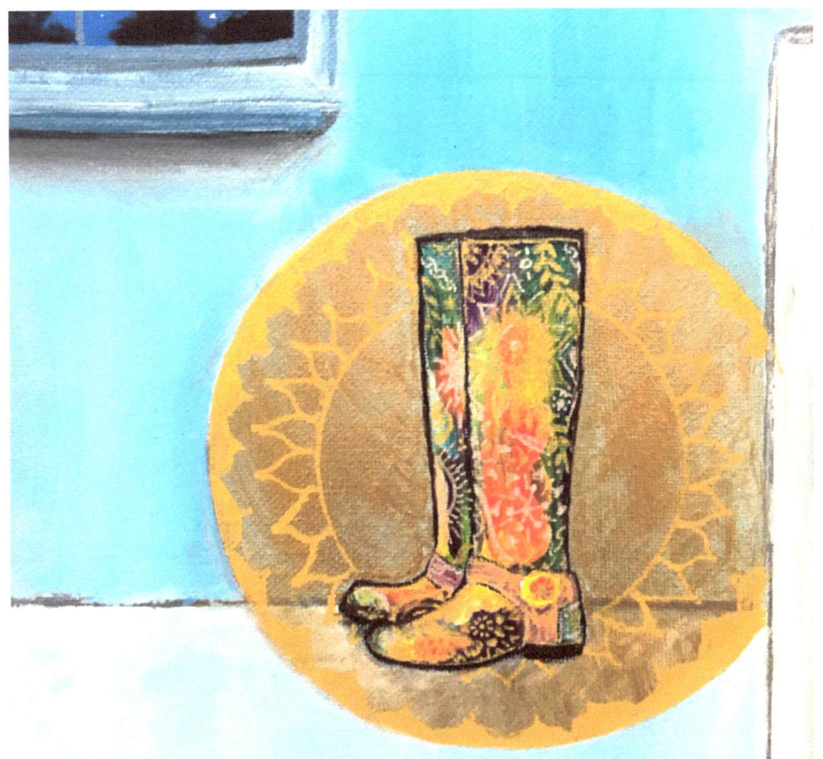

The light rippled out from a mysterious pair of dazzlingly colorful boots. Confounded, she stared at them, feeling a pleasant fluttering in her chest. They were the most beautiful shoes she had ever seen.

"We are the seven-league boots," a voice said from everywhere and nowhere. "We have come to take you on a journey to find the beauty you seek."

It took a few moments for Keira to comprehend what the voice had said.

"A... a journey? You want to take ME on a journey?" Keira was incredulous.

"Yes, my dear," said the boots. "We heard your call and we are here to help. There is absolutely nothing to fear."

Keira surveyed her room, so dull compared to the glistening glowing boots. Perhaps she had fallen asleep, and she was dreaming. Perhaps she could enjoy the dream.

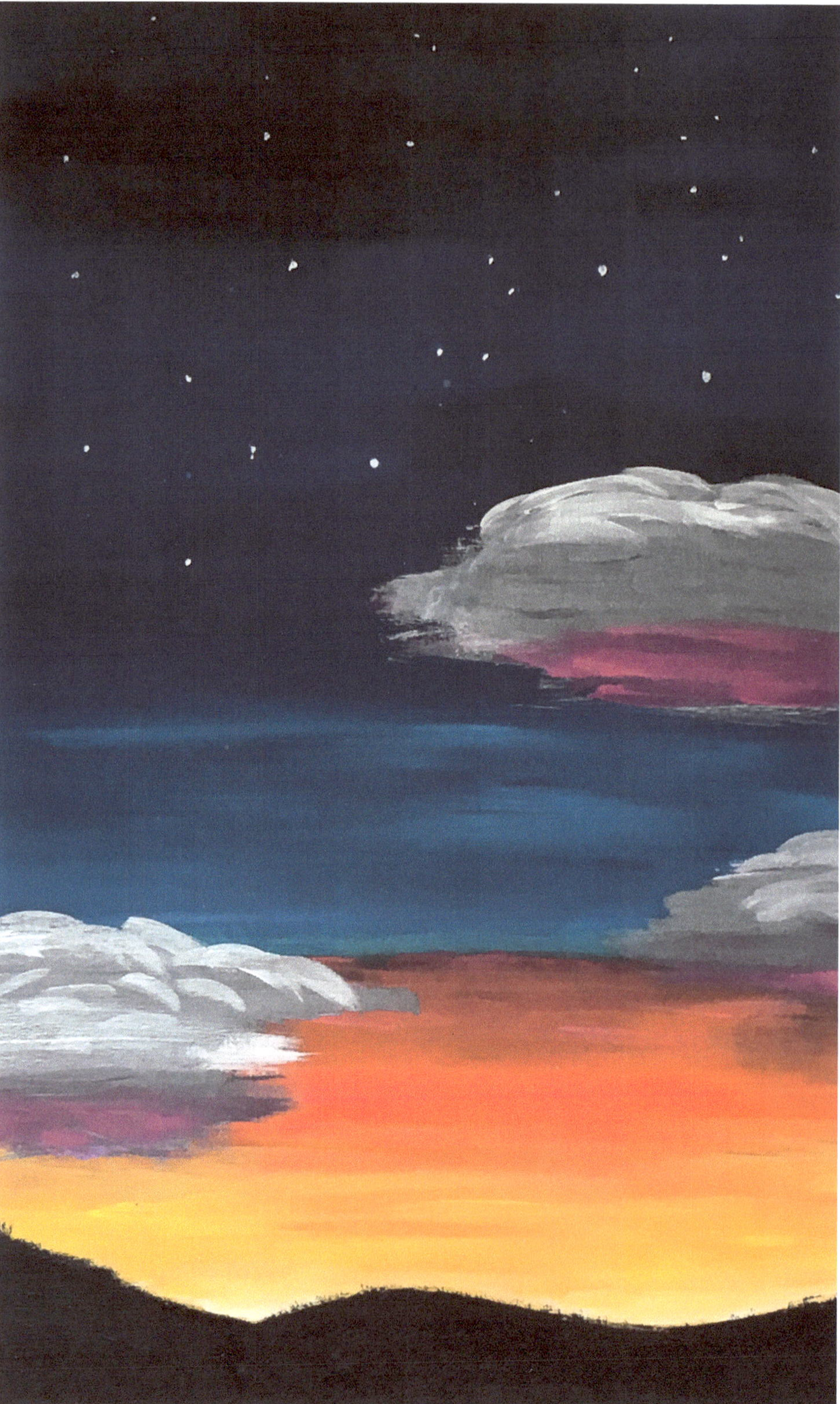

With that thought, the fluttering in her heart grew, but Keira was not alarmed. It felt so light, so good! One by one, she put the boots on her feet: they fit perfectly. They were colorful, warm, and soft, with a sturdy tread, exactly as she had imagined. Now their glow surrounded her.

She looked up from her feet to see that her bedroom wall had begun to dematerialize. It was as if she were looking through a cloudy pane of glass that became clearer by the minute. Looking to the east she saw that the sun had indeed begun to rise over the rolling hills.

"What kind of dream is this?" she gasped, a bit dizzy from the sudden change in view.

"You are not dreaming," the boots said gently. "This is a portal to another realm, one that is very close to yours, but can only be seen by a few. Most children can see glimmers of it, but they lose the ability as adults. We bring the gift of travel through this realm: with just one step you can cover seven leagues (or twenty-one miles). Together we can explore the wonders of the earth in the span of a day."

Keira let those words sink in: she could see the entire world in a day? The obligations and responsibilities of her ordinary life paled in comparison to the possibility of this wondrous journey.

Taking a deep breath, she said, "I am ready."

"Take the first step," said the boots. "Let your heart guide the way."

Feeling drawn to the warmth of the sun to the east, Keira stepped through the space where her bedroom wall had been. It was marvelous! She felt tall, as tall as the house, but she was aware of every small detail around her, like the texture of moss on a nearby flowerpot.

The boots had spoken true: when she walked, she moved at a dizzying pace. She quickly left the streetlights of her neighborhood behind her, passing highways, then country roads. The houses became sparse, until she could see nothing but trees.

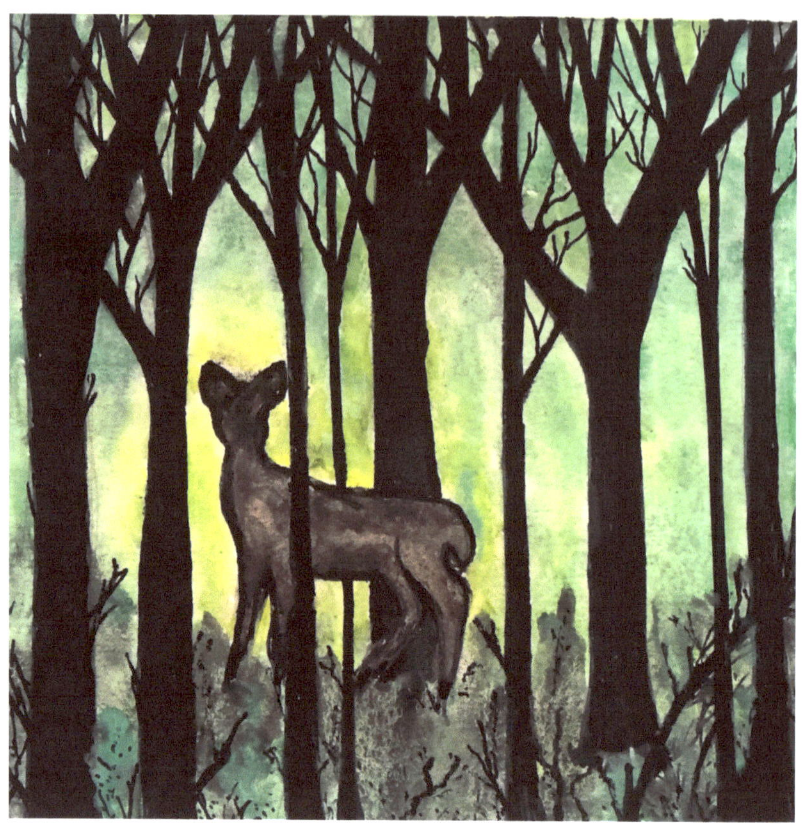

Keira moved deftly through the quiet forest. No thorns jumped up to tangle her feet, no hidden ditches threw her off-balance. She felt as if she were gliding effortlessly, following a path that only made sense to her.

Bunnies and squirrels darted across her path. Off in the distance she glimpsed the outline of a deer weaving its own way through the early morning light.

"Can the animals see me?" she asked the boots.

"Yes, they can," the boots replied. "They also share this realm."

On she walked, deeper into the forest, where the trees grew larger and farther apart. Clearings gave way to dazzling vistas of rolling hills as the sun climbed ever higher in the sky. She had never seen sunlight like this before: its light was as brilliant and prismatic as the shoes she wore. It was as if she could see the web that wove the sky.

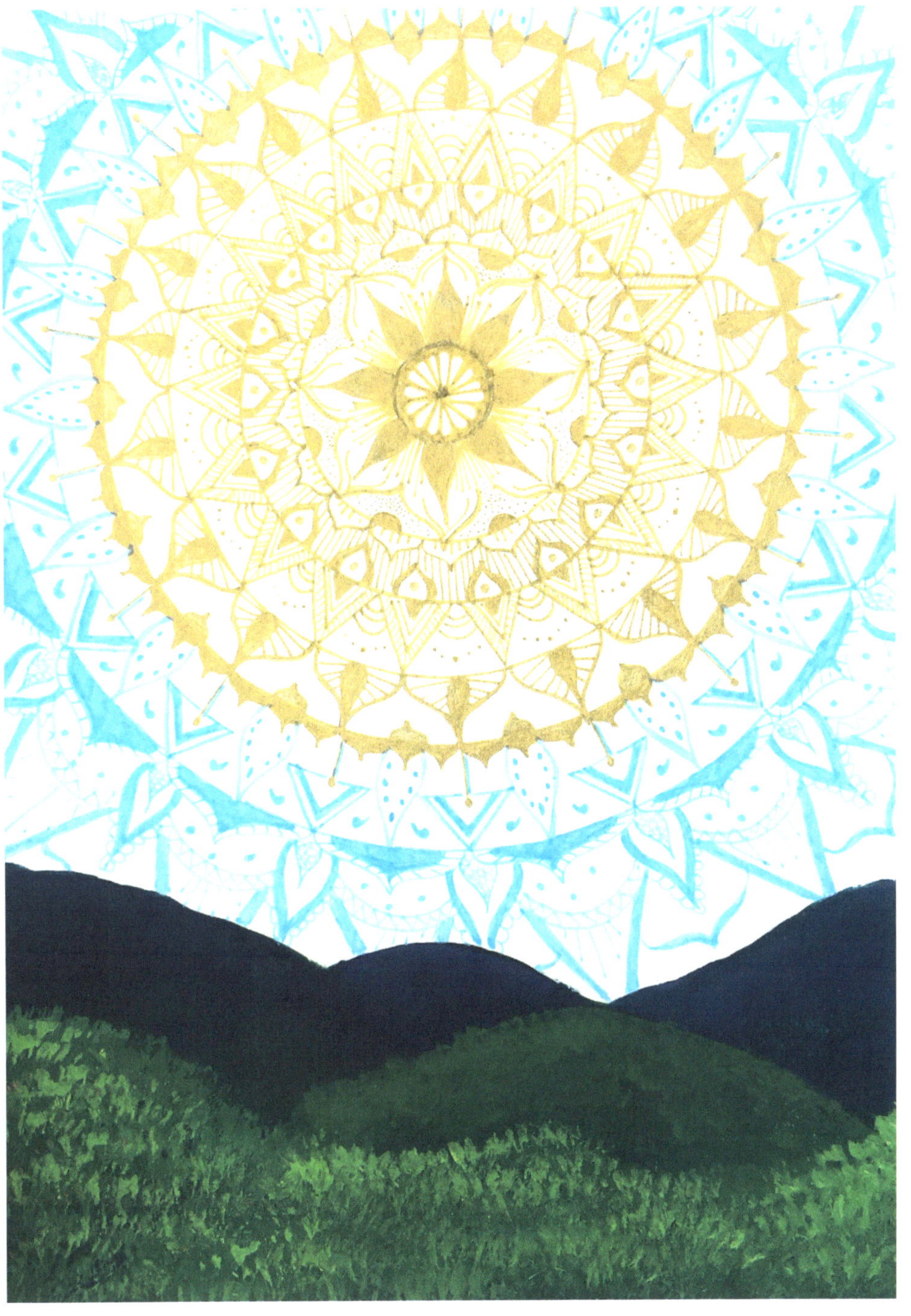

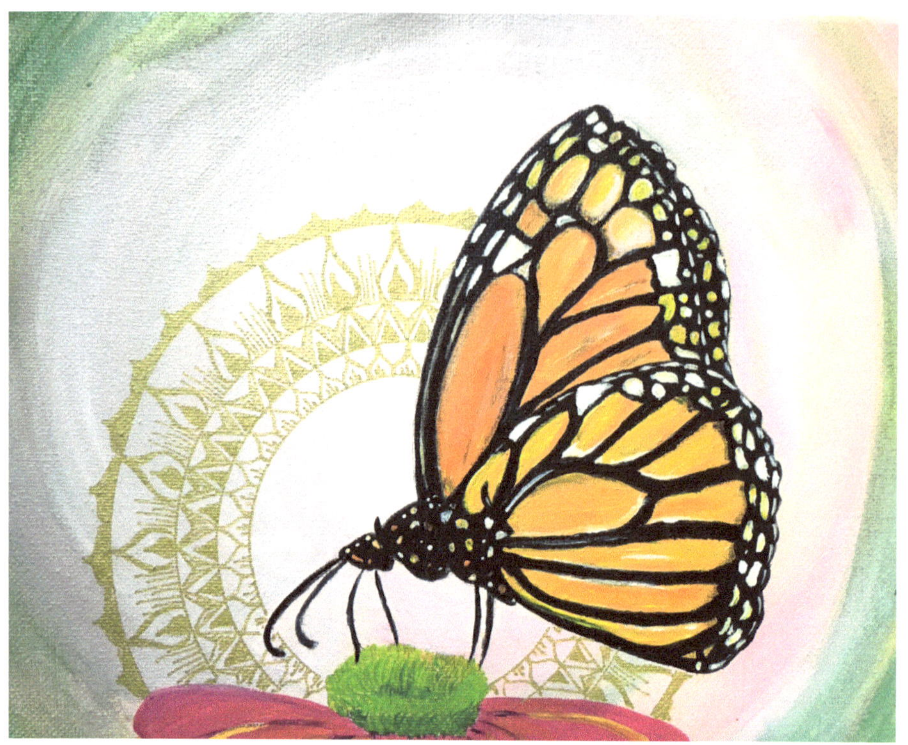

On the edge of a meadow, Keira spied a butterfly visiting each flower. She slowed her pace to watch him work. Unlike ordinary butterflies, this one had a sphere of light radiating out from its body, just like the boots on her feet and the sun in the sky.

"Why are you glowing?" she mused aloud. "What is this strange and beautiful light I see?"

"Why, it's my essence, of course" replied the butterfly. "Everyone has one!"

Keira blinked in surprise that the butterfly had responded.

"But I've never seen it on any other butterfly," she retorted.

"I dunno lady. Maybe you weren't really looking. Gotta go, lots of flowers to see!" The butterfly turned his back fluttered away, leaving Keira stunned.

"If everyone has one, why don't I?" Keira mused, looking down at her chest. The boots were silent.

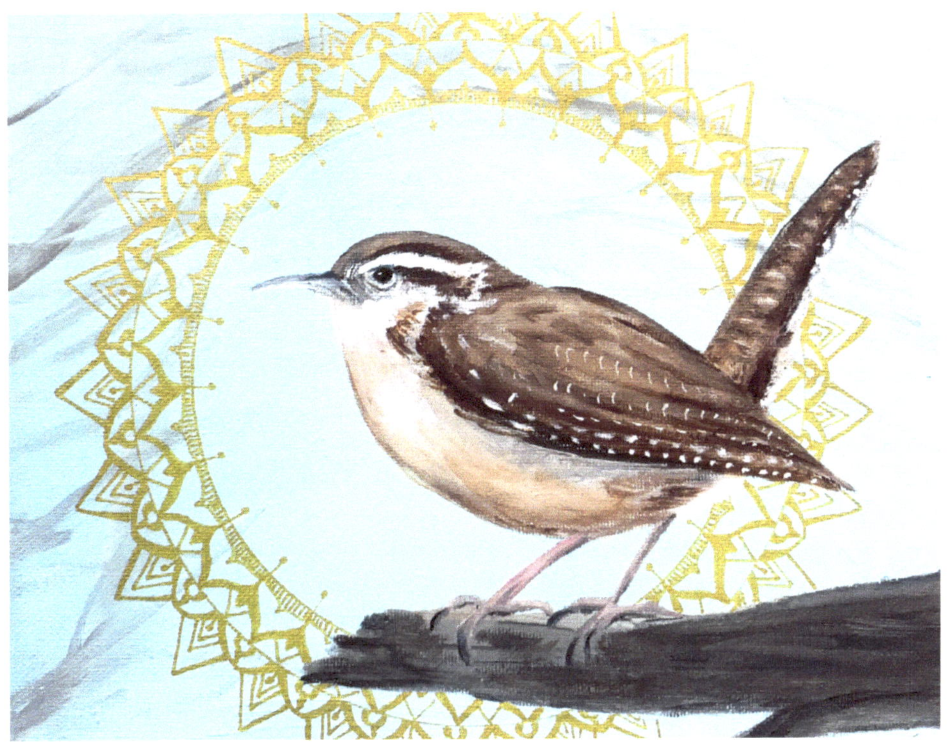

Back into the forest she went, pondering what it meant to see someone's essence. Under the shadow of the great canopy, she heard a rustling in some underbrush nearby.

"Cheep-a-duh! Cheep-a-duh!" a loud voice rang out.

Keira scanned the twigs and thorns until she saw a golden light bobbing about, surrounding a tiny brown bird.

"Hello, little bird. My name is Keira." Perhaps it would be good to introduce herself this time.

"Oh, hello, Keira. I am Wren." Perched on a dried twig, the bird's dancing halo was even clearer and more brilliant.

"I was just admiring your essence," Keira said to Wren.

"Why, thank you," replied Wren. "But I must be going, no time to dawdle!" And just like that, Wren was off, hidden in the underbrush.

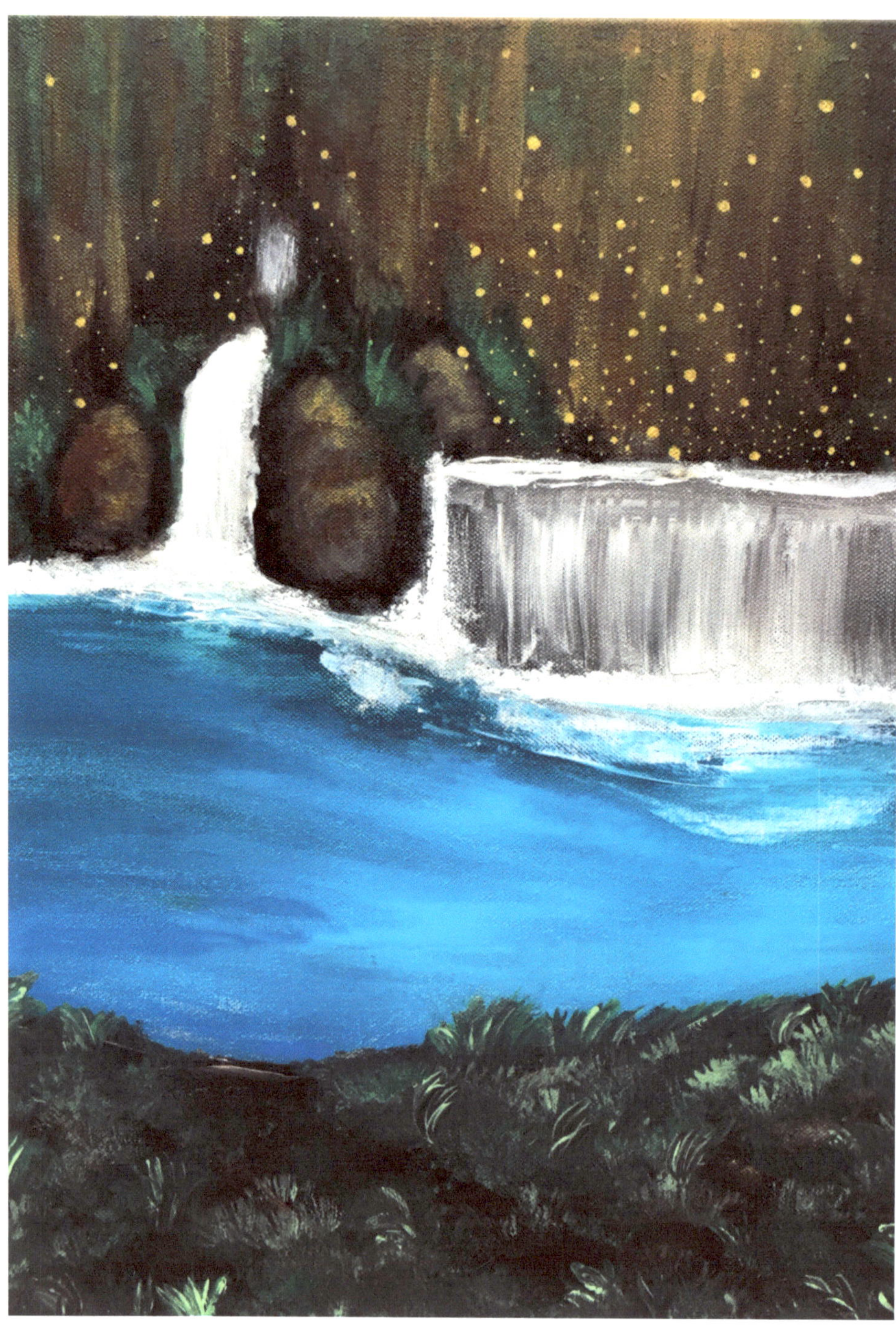

Keira wandered on, following the sound of a babbling brook. One by one, little trickles joined forces with the brook until water was rushing over rocks and pouring into pools.

A feeling of deep peace settled over her and she paused to rest on a large boulder by the stream. Hundreds of insects hovered by the water, each shining with their own golden light. It reminded Keira of summer evenings when she was a child, watching the fireflies and imagining that they were fairies. How could she have lost touch with this sense of awe?

She sat in reverie for quite some time until the boots spoke once more.

"What else does your heart want to see?"

A million ideas flooding into Keira's mind, so many that she feared she could never decide. For a moment she froze, worried that she would make the wrong choice. But the boots had asked about her heart: what did ***it*** want to see?

Focusing on her heart, she asked again. Clear as a bell, the answer came. "Follow the water," it said. "We must go to the sea."

Yes, the sea! Keira's whole body leapt at the idea of visiting the ocean. "Thank you!" she said to the boots, and to her heart, and she began to walk once more.

Miles and miles, she hiked along the rushing stream until it became a river. The land flattened and the trees thinned. Farmland appeared, then disappeared, as the rich earth became sandy and salty. Soon there were only spiky palms and sea grasses on dunes.

The sun was low in the sky when she arrived at the vast ocean. Keira had never seen such a beautiful sunset.

Standing on the shoreline, Keira longed to keep going, to walk right into the sea.

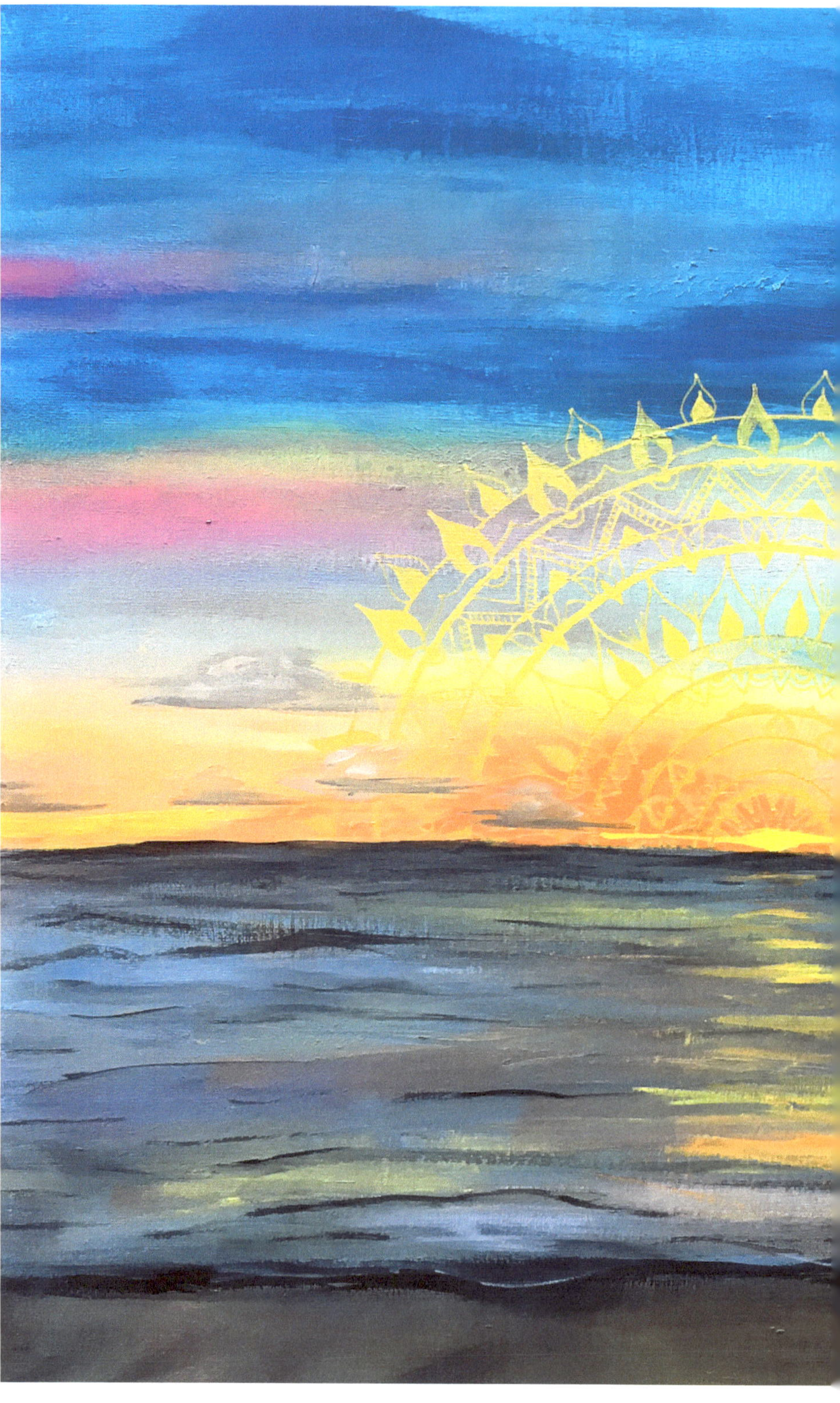

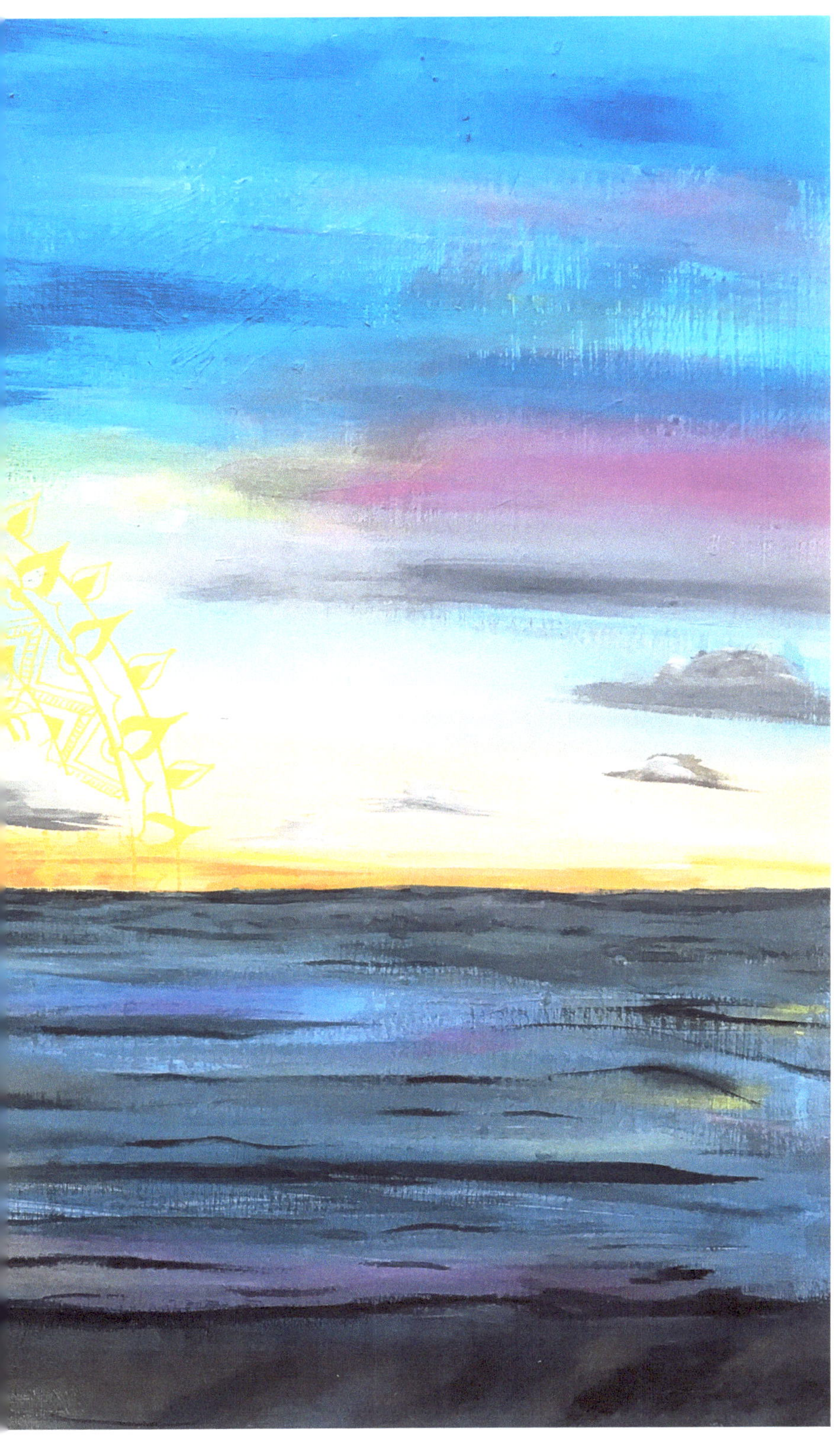

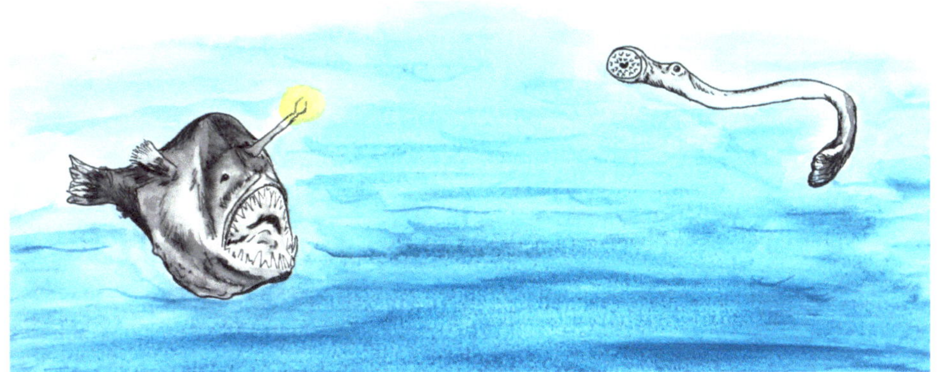

"Is it possible?" she asked the boots. "Can I walk into the water safely?"

"Yes," they assured her. "The rules of this realm are different than yours. You may go anywhere you please, even into the ocean."

With a smile on her face, Keira strode into the depths of the sea.

At first, all she perceived was darkness. Once her eyes adjusted she began to see movement all around her as she strode along the sea floor. She had no trouble breathing underwater, and though she felt the coolness of the water, she was not uncomfortable or cold.

The farther she went, the more she began to worry about the monsters that lurked here in the deep. What if they weren't as friendly as the butterfly and the wren? She shuddered as an eel with a mouthful of teeth slithered by in the distance.

"Keep going," said the boots. Or was it her heart that was speaking?

She looked more closely at a shadow swimming by. She thought she saw a golden light, even here in the night-black water. Yes, indeed, it was an angler fish, a tiny light aglow in front of it! It was comforting to know that all creatures, even the scary-looking ones, had their own beautiful essence.

The angler fish suddenly turned and swam away from her, as if startled. The water behind her did seem to be brighter and warmer, so Keira turned around, just in time for a majestic sight.

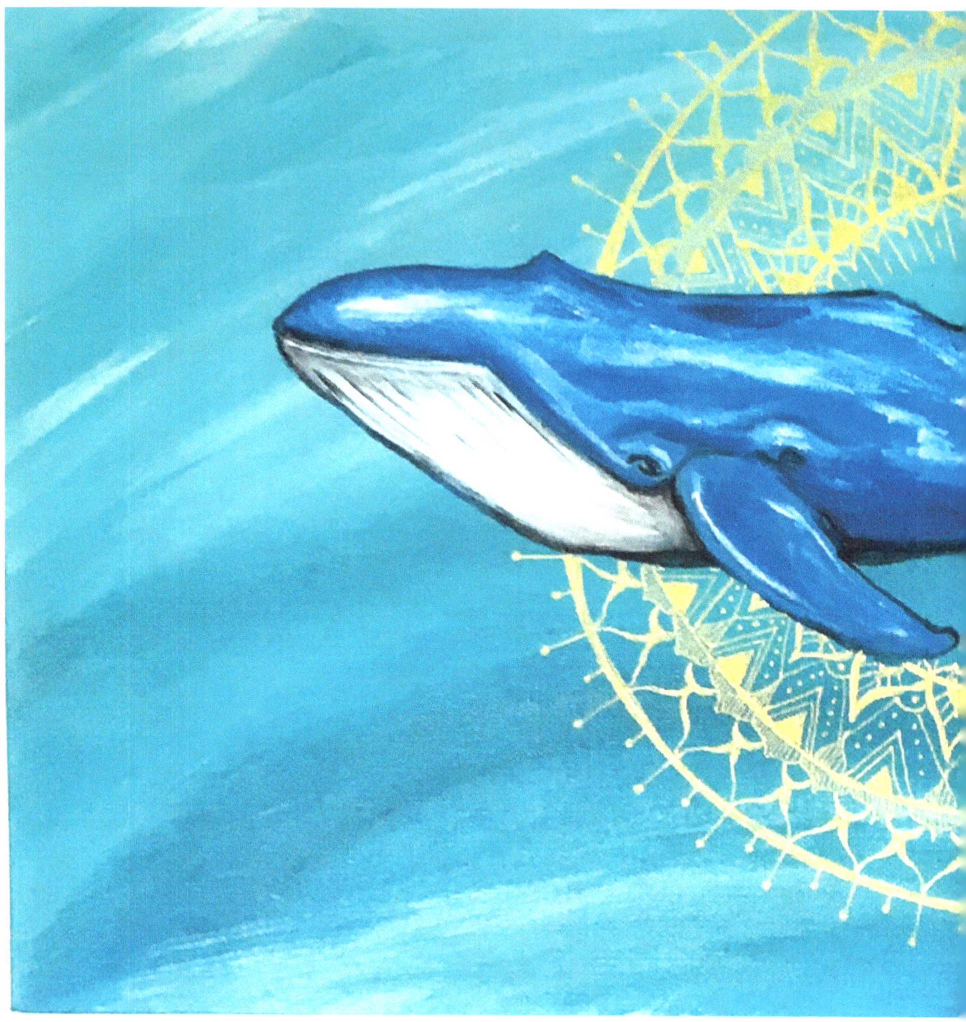

Keira had read about whales, but this one was more immense than she could have ever imagined. Its halo of gold was the size of a small building and lit up the water around them as bright as day.

"Hello!" Keira exclaimed. "I'm so glad to meet you!"
"Hello, little one," the whale turned and replied. I have not seen your kind in the depths for many years."

"You've seen humans down here before?" Keira asked, surprised.

"Your kind used to visit us to learn the wisdom of the deep. It has been ever so long since one made the trip." The whale's tone was melancholic. "We wondered if the ability had been lost entirely."

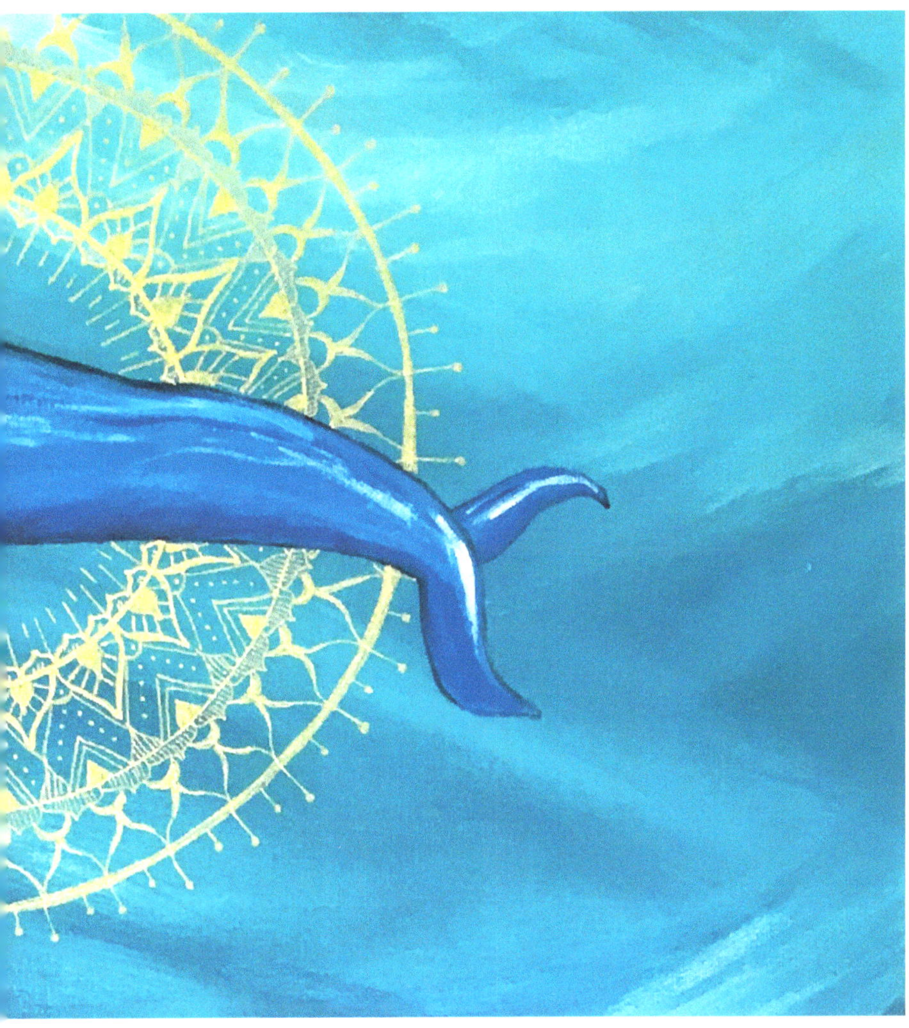

"I am only here because of the boots," Keira replied, gesturing to the multi-colored glow at her feet.

"Well, I am glad you are here, little one," the whale's voice boomed. "It gives me hope for the world above."

Keira and the whale swapped stories until fatigue washed over her.

"I think it is time for me to go home," she told the whale. "You wouldn't believe the day I've had!"

"Farewell, brave traveler," the whale said. "We will remember you." He swam away, taking his light with him.

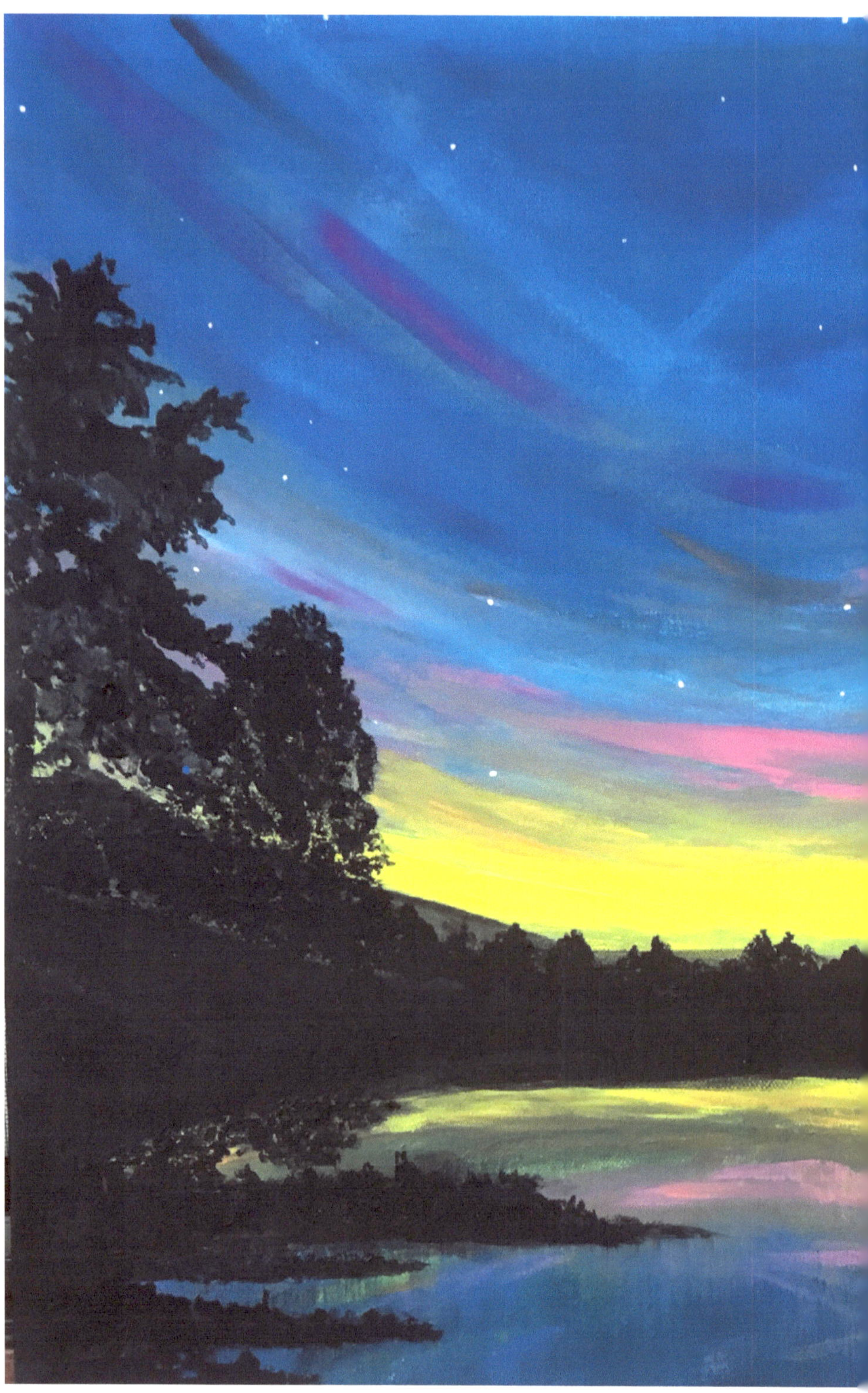

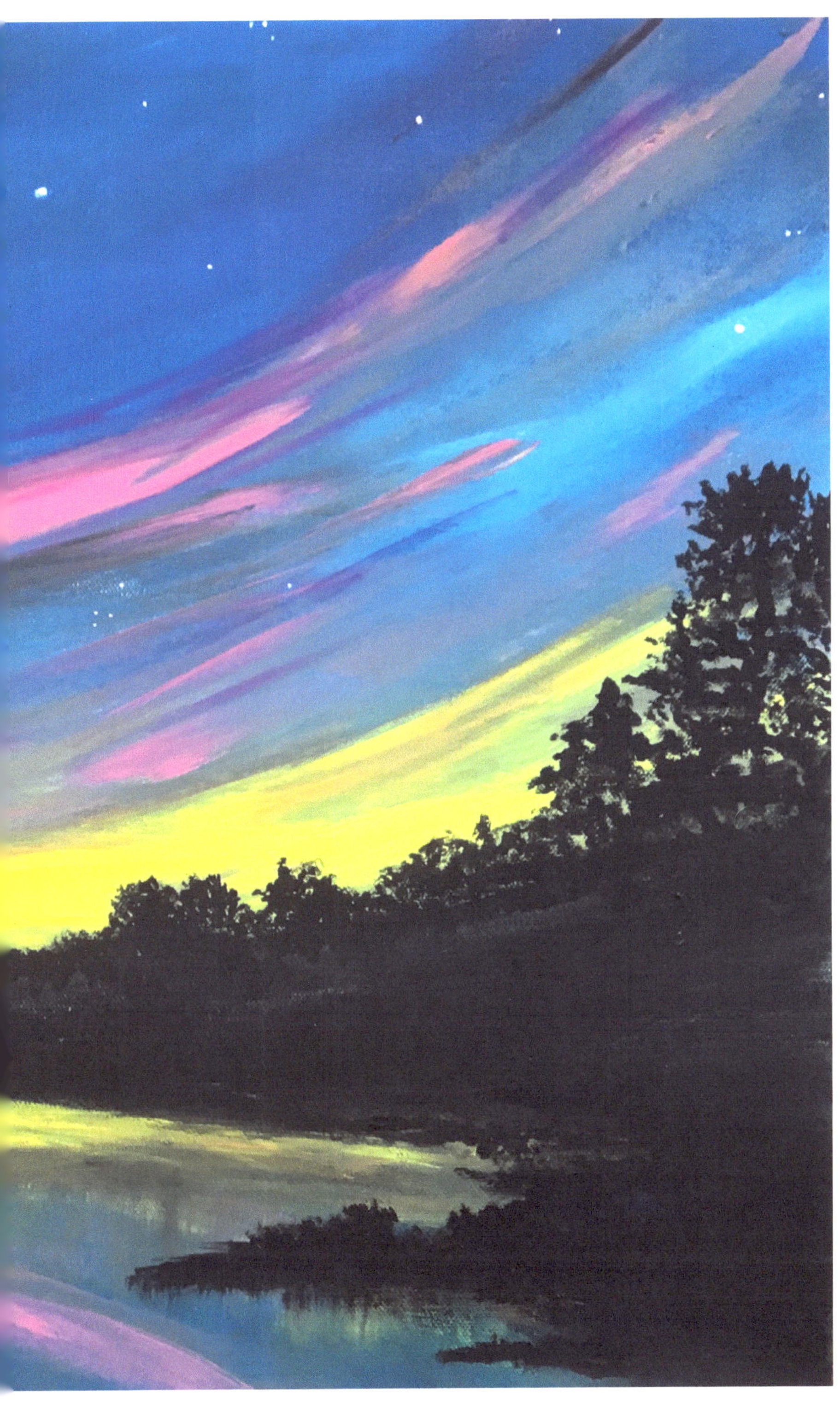

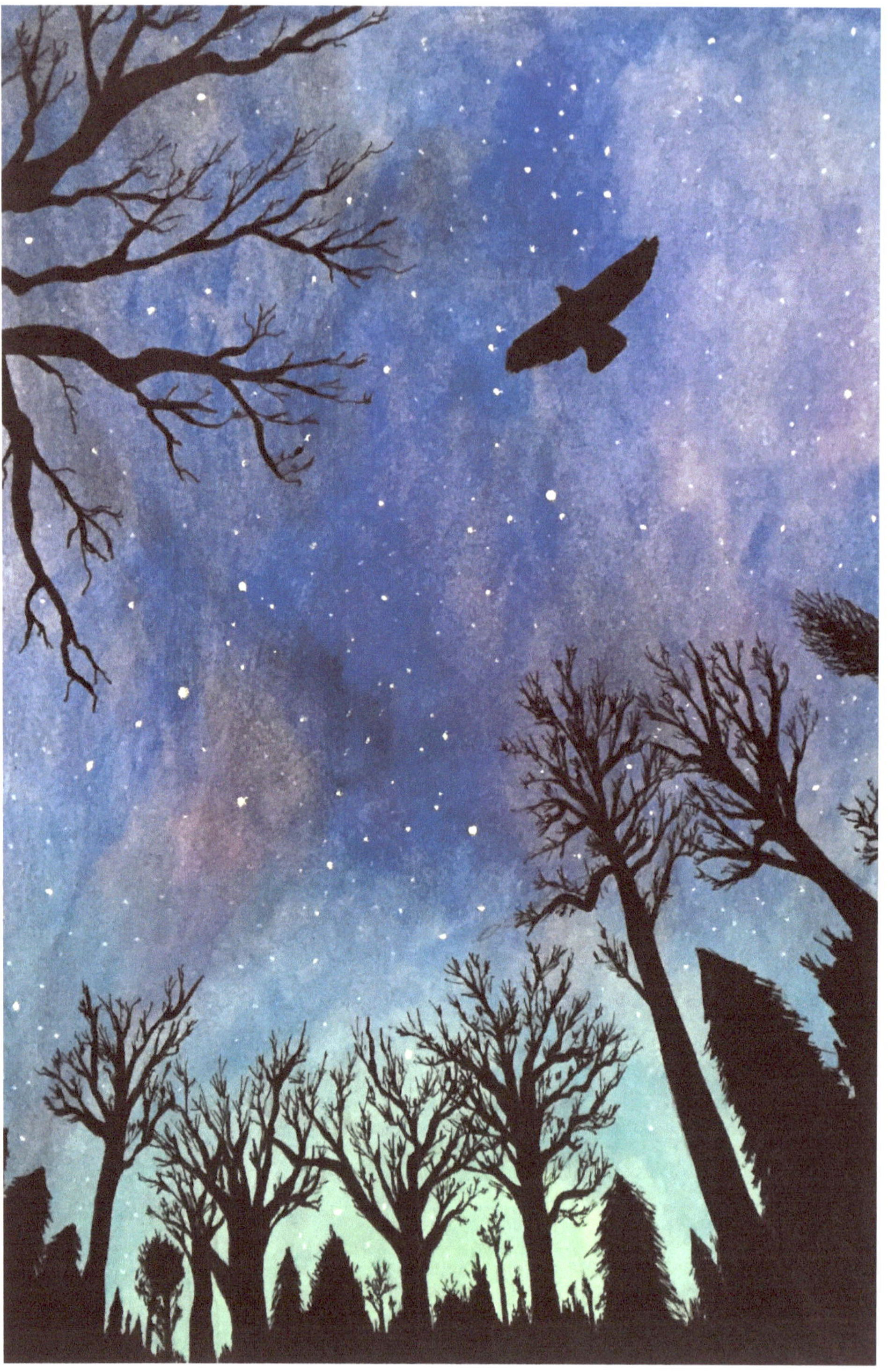

Keira followed the direction of her heart toward home, and swiftly headed back on shore.

Retracing her steps, Keira walked along the river, back through the farmlands, and up into the highlands. Shrubs and saplings gave way to pine trees, then sturdy oaks. Although it felt like she had spent hours underwater with the whale, daylight had not yet faded from the sky above.

Soon she was back in the dense forest and following a meandering stream.

Her day had been filled with such beauty and magic. She could hardly believe it was almost done. She wasn't sure she wanted to go back home, to her ordinary life.

Guided by the soft light of the moon, Keira climbed ridges and walked through valleys. The paths were becoming more familiar, and she could spot houses off in the distance. With each step she was getting closer to the mundane world where her journey had begun.

Ahead of her a golden light emerged from the dark forest. A stately buck slowly made its way toward her. She paused, and let it approach.

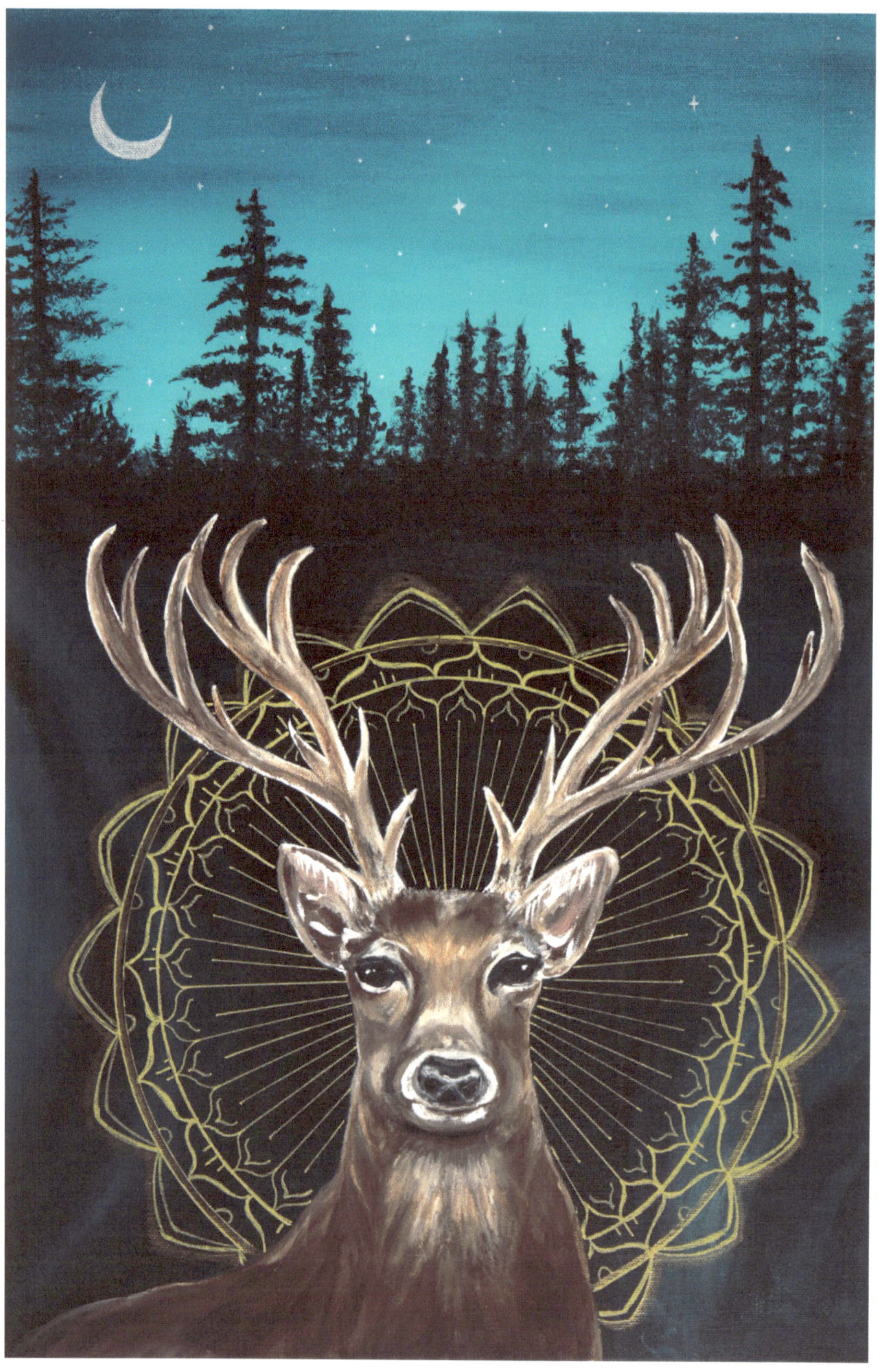

"Hello, deer." she said softly.

"Good evening," answered the buck. The golden light of his aura blazed in the soft night air.

"I have seen a thousand deer but never one like you," she told him.

"Of course not," he responded incredulously. "Like humans, every deer is special."

He paused. "But not every human walks the paths in-between like you do."

"I... I have been given a gift by these boots," she pointed downward. "They allow me to see the world as never before. I can see your light, your essence. It is spectacular."

And then the truth spilled out. "I don't want to go back to the way things were," she confessed.

The deer looked at her in silence for a long moment.

"Humans can walk these paths whenever they want. The ability is only lost in those who do not use it."

Warm tears of joy pooled in Keira's eyes as she considered a future full of days like today.

"Thank you!" she said, as she bowed to the deer in gratitude.

The deer bowed its antlers in return, and then ambled off into the trees.

"Let's go home," Keira told the boots.

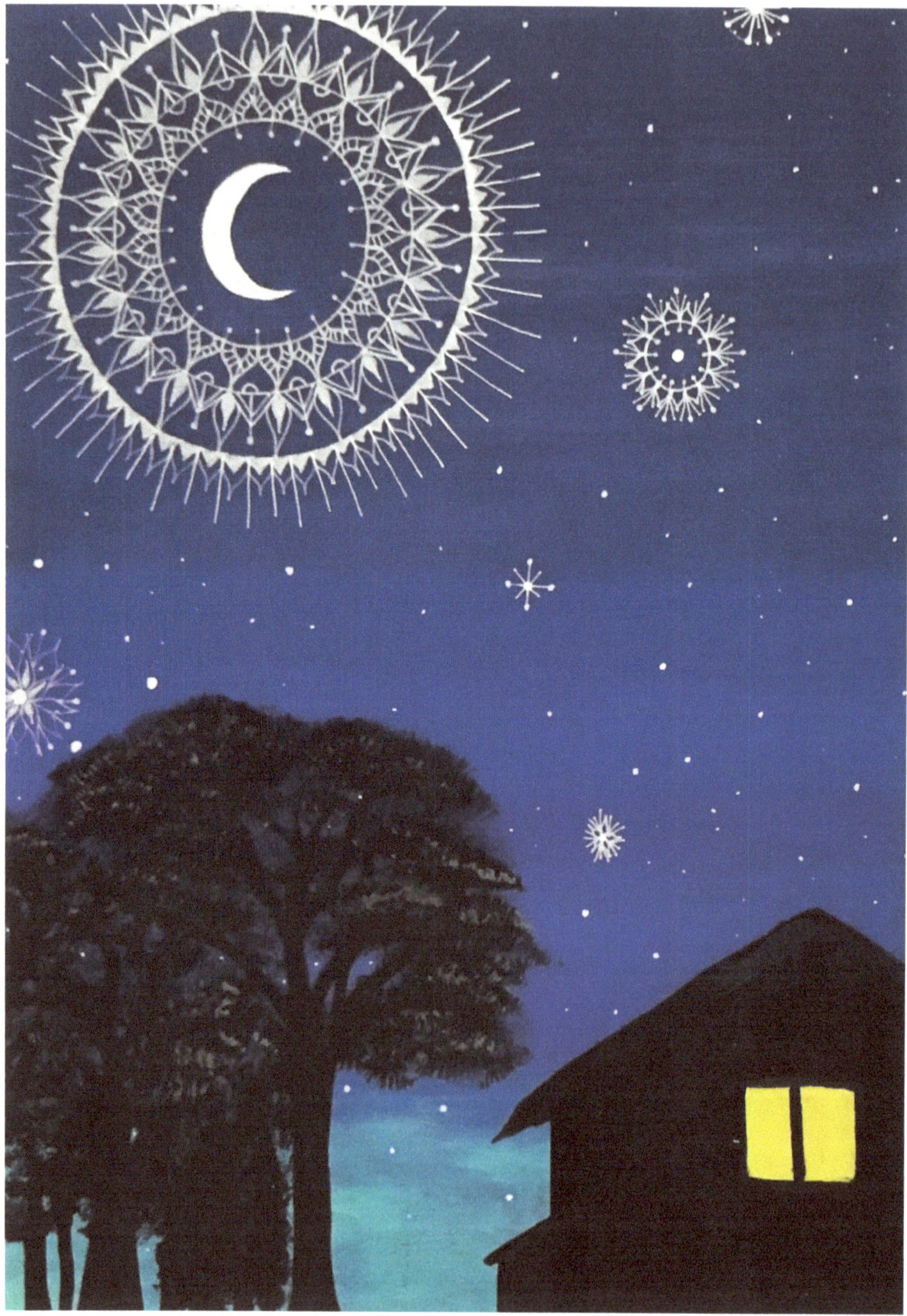

Out of the forest she walked, across the roads and highways, until orderly neighborhoods were popping up all around her. Shopping malls and street lights lit her way back to the little street on which she lived. There was her house, just as she'd remembered it.

"Home," she thought, imagining the cozy warmth in the yellow glow of her kitchen window.

Her home was not exactly the same, however, for around the old familiar moon was a lacy mandala of sacred geometry. The stars and planets showed off their style as well.

Keira drank in the view and promised herself to never again lose sight of such beauty. It would make every day - and every night - special.

She looked down at herself and saw the dazzling light of the boots radiating out from her feet. In all this joy, she still felt one last pang of fear. "I have seen the essence of so many creatures, and even that of sky above. But I see nothing when I look at myself: only the magic of the boots. Do I have this beauty inside of me? What if I don't?"

"It's time to step back into your life and find out," was all the boots would say.

Keira decided not to dwell on regret after such a perfect day. She nodded and walked around the house to her bedroom wall, which was still transparent and open.

There was her lamp, her closet, her bed. The pillows looked particularly inviting, and she stifled a yawn as she stepped inside.

She slowly removed the boots.

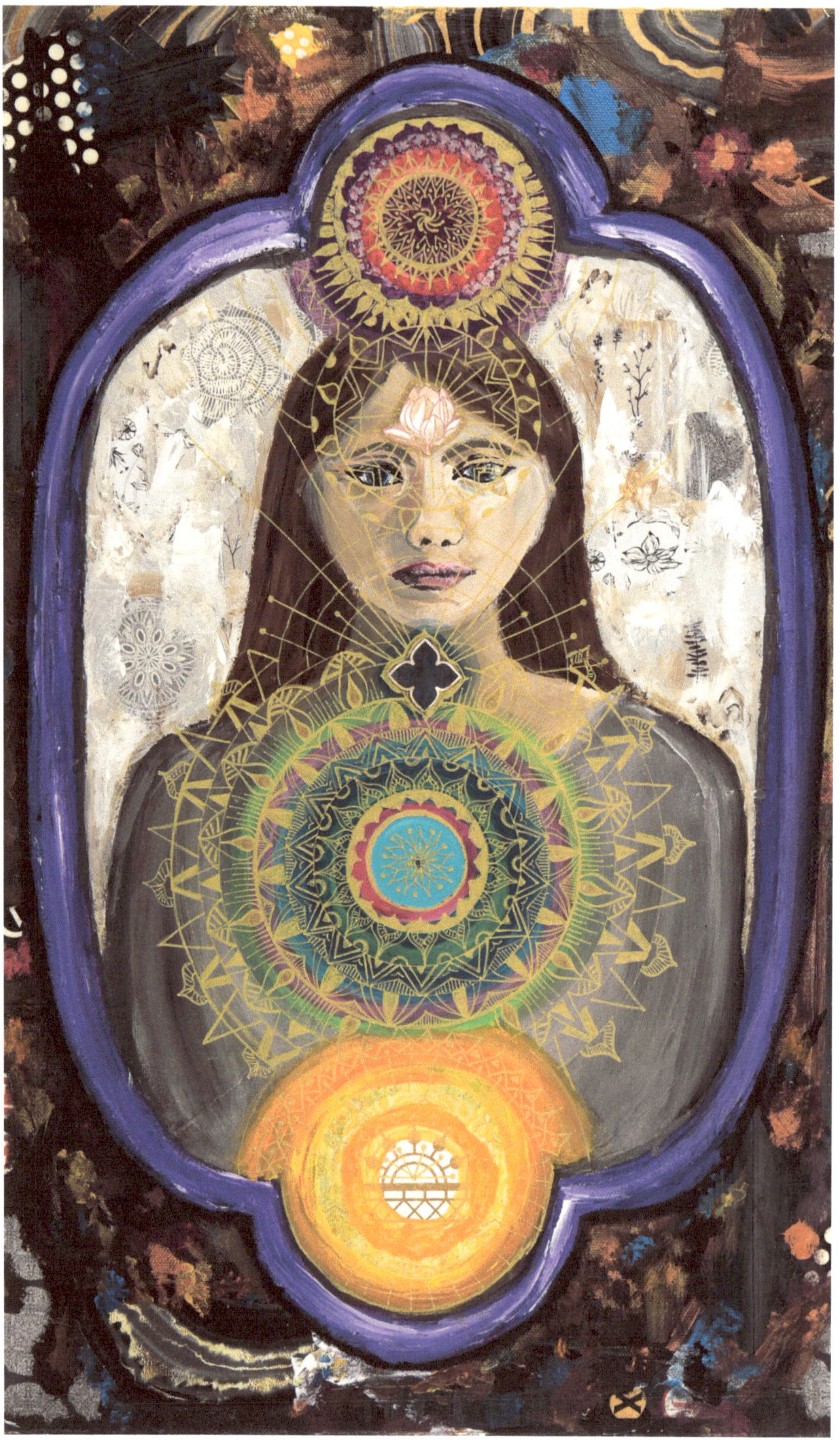

As she set them aside, the light immediately shifted in the room.

"Good-bye for now!" said the boots.

They disappeared in the blink of an eye, taking their glow with them. The bedroom wall in front of her began to flicker into being and become solid once more. The patterns of the landscape merged with the texture of the wall and even with the boots gone, Keira could still see bright colors shifting and spinning around her.

Squinting, she looked straight ahead. There seemed to be another figure in her room with her: one shadowed by all the dazzling lights between them.

"Hello?" she whispered. There was no response.

She stepped closer to the figure but stubbed her toe against the hardening wall.

It was her mirror! She was standing in front of her mirror: the colorful shadow was HER!

Astonishment turned to glee as she realized she could see her own essence after all. Chakras of color wheeled before her in all of her favorite colors.

The gift really was hers to keep. She would never again be the same after this magical day. She had seen the light of the world, but more importantly, she could see her own light.

“Life cannot be dreary,” she thought, “when such magic is available to us.”

Keira slept deeply that night and revisited all of her new friends in her dreams. The next day she rose with the sun and went out to visit the birds. And though the changes she made each day after that were small, her life had changed drastically and irrevocably. She was no longer haunted by sleepless nights and dreary days. She was in love with herself, and her world.

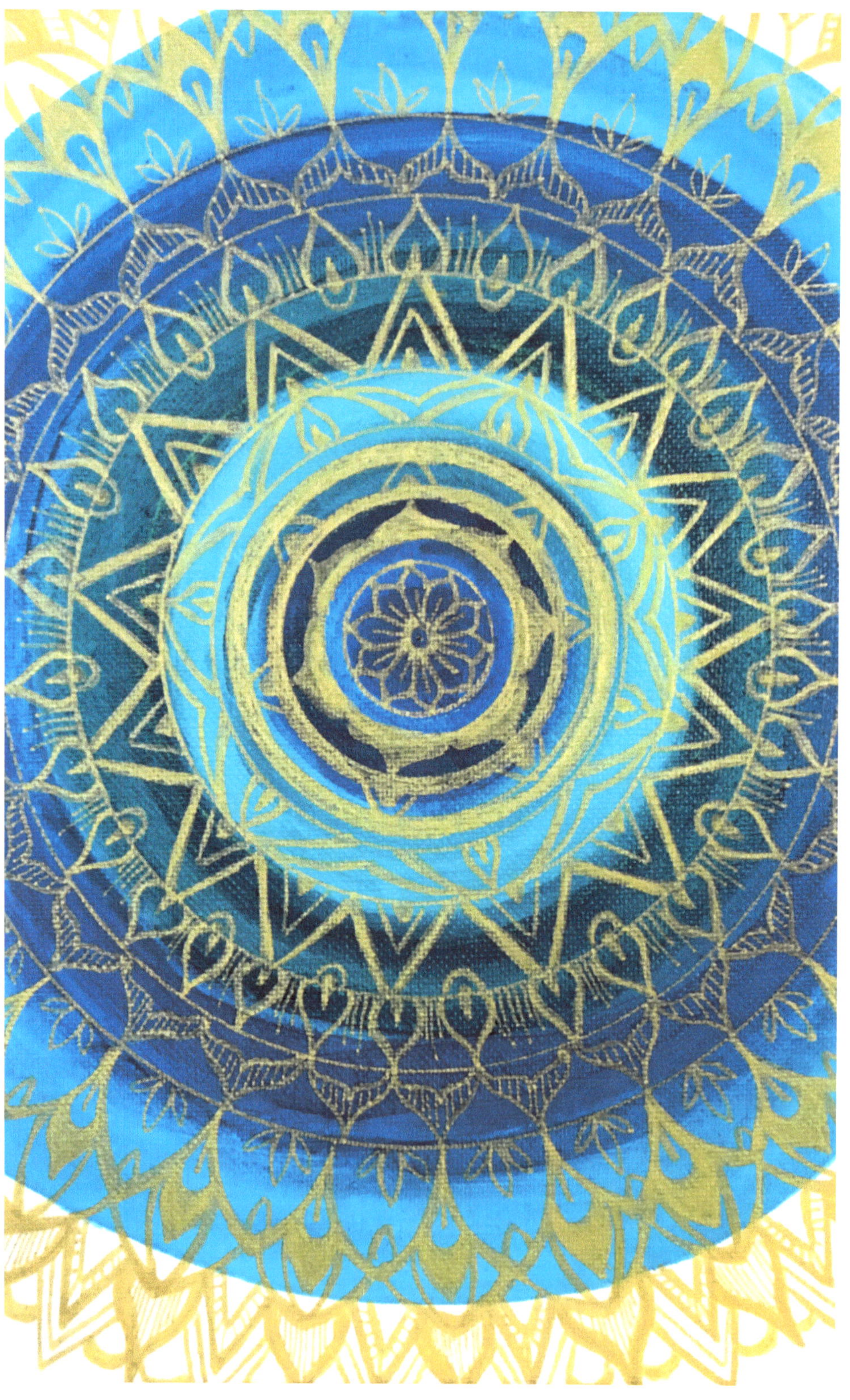

Dedication

This story is for my fellow seekers: the lost ones, the wayfinders, the orphans, and the beloved ones. May you always find magic on your path and leave beauty in your wake. I love you. I love us.

To Brandon and Eliza:
my friends, my patrons, and my
quarantine FaceTime lifeline.
Thank you for being you.

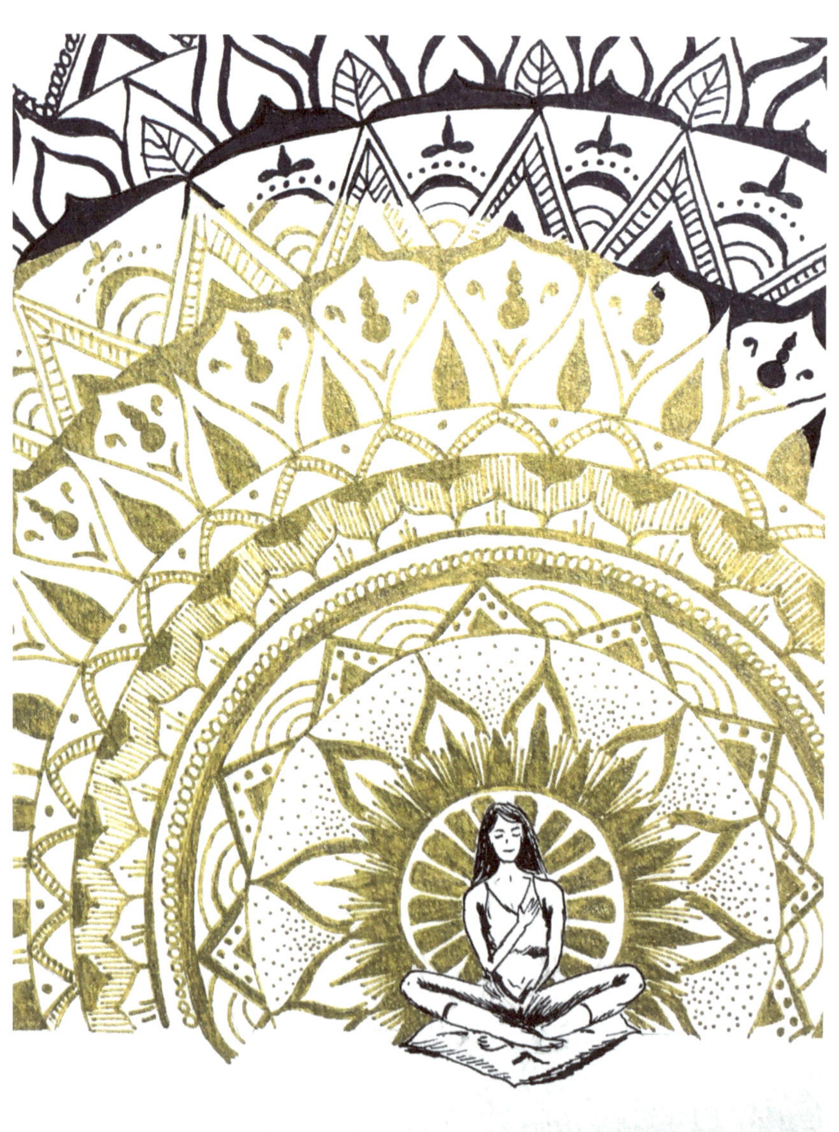

About This Book

In my life coaching training with Martha Beck, I was introduced to a powerful meditation called "The Seven-League Boots." I have used it many times for myself and for clients as a way to find clarity in times of stress.

The paintings came first, in random order, but each time I finished one I knew they were part of the same story. Eventually I realized that I was painting a journey like the one in the meditation and I filled in the gaps as needed. I invented Keira to stand in for all of us and chose her name because it sounds like the cry of the red-tailed hawk.

I hope the book brings you a sense of joy and possibility. Thank you for spending some of your precious time with me.

Dana Wheeles
12/2020

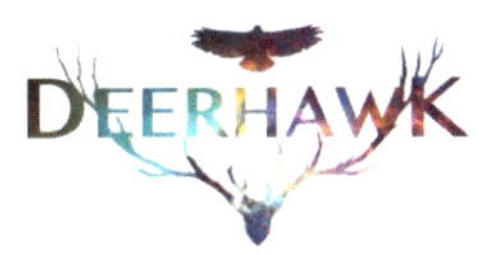

Deerhawk Art Studio
www.deerhawkhealing.com

www.ingramcontent.com/pod-product-compliance
Lightning Source LLC
LaVergne TN
LVHW071629100826
845154LV00005BA/114
* 9 7 8 1 7 3 6 6 0 1 5 0 1 *